FOR EMILY, TOMMY, AND DANNY
K. M.

TO MY MUSEUM FRIENDS, MAX AND LUCA
H. R.

Text copyright © 2017 by Kate Messner
Illustrations copyright © 2017 by Heather Ross

First edition 2017

Library of Congress Catalog Card Number 2017942647
ISBN 978-0-7636-7846-3

18 19 20 21 22 CCP 10 9 8 7 6 5 4 3

Printed in Shenzhen, Guangdong, China

This book was typeset in Minion.
The illustrations were created digitally.

Candlewick Press
99 Dover Street
Somerville, Massachusetts 02144

visit us at www.candlewick.com

CONTENTS

CHAPTER 1
FIELD TRIP DAY . . . AND FERGUS, TOO!

FERGUS LOVED being the class pet in Miss Maxwell's room. He loved everything about school, and he was good at following the class rules.

When Miss Maxwell said, "Sit quietly for storytime," Fergus sat still and listened.

When Miss Maxwell said, "Follow the directions carefully," Fergus followed every step.

When the students solved math problems, Fergus solved them, too.
He always kept his eyes on his own work.

And when Miss Maxwell said, "It's
time to clean up," Fergus tidied his cage.

His favorite part of the day was music.
Fergus did a jazzy dance while the children
sang and played instruments.

One day, Miss Maxwell told the students they would be taking a field trip to the Museum of Natural History.

Everyone was excited. "I want to see the dinosaurs," said Emma.

"I want to see the butterfly garden," said Jake.

"I want to see the planetarium," said Lucy. "I want to wish on a shooting star!"

Fergus wanted to see all those things, too. What fun it would be to wish on a shooting star! He couldn't wait for the big trip.

But when field trip day arrived, Miss Maxwell said, "Emma, will you please give Fergus some sunflower seeds? We don't want him to be hungry while we are away."

Wait! Fergus thought. *Does that mean that I'm not going on the field trip?*

"Here you go, Fergus," Emma said. She put the seeds in his cage. "Sorry you can't come to the museum with us."

Why can't I go to the museum? Fergus thought. He did everything with Miss Maxwell's class. He was sure there must be some mistake. So he packed his lunch to go.

He combed his soft mouse fur so he would look nice for the trip. He waited for Miss Maxwell to notice. He waited for her to say, "What a great museum mouse Fergus will be! We must take him along on our field trip."

But Miss Maxwell was busy taking attendance and getting the first-aid kit ready and watching for the bus. The children were busy remembering lunches and zipping coats and lining up. No one paid any attention to Fergus.

I want to go on the field trip, too! Fergus thought. *I want to see the dinosaurs and butterflies. I want to wish on a shooting star!*

So when no one was watching, he slipped out of his cage and hid in Emma's backpack.

Emma picked it up and carried it out to the bus.

"We're going on a field trip to the museum!" Emma told the bus driver.

And deep in the dark of the backpack,
Fergus smiled. He was going on the field
trip, too.

CHAPTER 2
FERGUS FINDS A BUDDY

"There's plenty of room for everyone," Miss Maxwell said as they boarded the bus. "Please sit with your field trip buddy and stay in your seats until we get to the museum."

Oh, dear, Fergus thought. *Who will be my field trip buddy?* He was the only class pet. All the children had already paired up.

So Fergus found a buddy in Emma's backpack. Sort of.

The bus ride to the museum was bumpy. Fergus and his buddy bounced all around.

When the bus went around a sharp curve, Fergus held on to his buddy for dear life. When the bus drove over a bump, Fergus and his buddy went flying. Then they landed —*plop!*— right on Emma's ham sandwich.

Finally, the bus stopped. Fergus peeked out of Emma's backpack and saw a big building.

"We're here! Line up with your buddy," Miss Maxwell said. "Don't forget your lunch!"

And don't forget me! Fergus thought.

Emma didn't. She carried him off the bus and into the museum.

Fergus stared at the enormous lobby. "Wow, look at this!" he told his buddy. It was the most amazing place he'd ever seen.

"This is where we will line up to get on the bus at the end of our visit," Miss Maxwell said. "Remember to look but don't touch today. Keep an eye out for your buddy, and be *sure* to stay with the group."

"Welcome to the Museum of Natural History," a tour guide said. "Please leave your backpacks in the coatroom. Then we will explore the museum."

Oh, no! thought Fergus. He did not want to stay with the coats. He wanted to explore. He wanted to see rocks and minerals. He wanted to see dinosaurs and butterflies. He wanted to wish on a shooting star.

Fergus watched the students leave. He wanted to stay with the group, but his buddy wasn't coming.

Fergus pulled . . . and tugged . . . and pushed with all his might.

His buddy stayed put.

"Come on!" Fergus cried.

"What's wrong?" someone asked.

Fergus turned around. There was another mouse, just his size.

"I can't explore the museum without a buddy," Fergus said. "But my buddy doesn't want to explore."

"Then come with me," the other mouse said. "My name is Zeke. I live here. I'll show you around."

So Fergus climbed down from the backpack and set off with his new buddy, Zeke, to explore.

MOON ROCK

CHAPTER 3
SPACE ROCKS, BUTTERFLIES, AND TROUBLE!

The first exhibit hall was full of rocks and minerals. There were shiny rocks and sparkly rocks. There were lumpy rocks and pointy rocks. Some of them came from faraway places. One came from outer space!

Fergus and Zeke scampered up onto a table to get a better look.

"Look!" Fergus said, pointing. "I see Jake and Lucy from school. And there's Emma!" He saw Miss Maxwell and the museum guide, too. They were leading the students into another room, behind a glass door.

"Where are they going?" Fergus asked. "We have to stay with the group!"

Fergus and Zeke squeezed through the door just before it closed.

The room on the other side was green and leafy. The air was warm and sweet-smelling. Bright flowers and fluttering butterflies were everywhere!

Fergus was so excited he did his jazzy dance. Butterflies flew all around him. He stopped dancing and stood as still as a mouse can be. Would a butterfly land on him? One came close enough to tickle his whiskers, but then it flew away to a flower.

"Come on!" Zeke called from the doorway. "This is only the beginning of our tour!"

There was so much to see at the museum! Fergus and Zeke followed Miss Maxwell's class from room to room. The hall of ocean life had a blue whale big enough to swallow the whole school bus.

One great hall was full of birds from all over the world. Another was full of reptiles. Fergus didn't care much for the snakes.

RATTLESNAKE

But he loved the room with big African animals.

"Come with me!" Zeke squeezed through a crack in the exhibit case and climbed up the lion's tail. "Now I'm the king of the beasts!"

"I don't think that's a good idea," Fergus said. "Miss Maxwell told the class, 'Look, but don't touch.'"

"Those are people rules!" Zeke balanced on the lion's ear. "We're mice!"

That was true, and playing on the lion looked like fun. So Fergus slipped into the exhibit case and climbed up to join Zeke. "Now we're both king of the beasts!" he squeaked.

Fergus and Zeke fluffed up their fur to look like manes. They roared as loud as they could.

They crept through the grass like tigers.

They beat their chests like gorillas.

They climbed all the way up the
elephant's tail. Then — *whoosh!* — they slid
down its bumpy trunk!

"Come on, Fergus," said Zeke. "The very best room is over here!"

Zeke led Fergus into a big, big room with funny-shaped sticks on the floor. Fergus walked right up to one. It was yellowy-white and rough. He sniffed it. It smelled very, very old.

"Follow me!" Zeke jumped up onto the stick. Fergus jumped up, too. The stick was connected to another stick.

And another. And another. Fergus and Zeke climbed higher and higher. How many sticks could there be?

Fergus looked up. He looked way, way, *way* up.

"It's a dinosaur!" Fergus said.

"And a playground!" Zeke said. "Come on!"

They played hide-and-seek in the maze of bones.

They climbed the duck-billed dinosaur and swung from his nose. *Whee!*

"Can't catch me!" Zeke shouted. So Fergus chased him.

They darted between foot bones. They climbed up leg bones. They climbed higher and higher, up hip bones, rib bones, and neck bones. Finally, they slipped inside a dinosaur's cool, shadowy mouth to rest.

"These teeth are very pointy," Fergus said, trying to catch his breath.

"That's because they belong to a Tyrannosaurus rex," Zeke said.

Fergus gulped. But when he worked up his courage and peered out from between the jagged teeth, he could see the whole huge dinosaur hall. The view was spectacular.

But Fergus couldn't see Miss Maxwell. He couldn't see Emma or Lucy or Jake or the tour guide. He'd been having so much fun, he'd forgotten to stay with the group!

Fergus jumped to the window and looked out. There was the school bus. It was ready to leave and take everyone home.

Everyone except Fergus.

CHAPTER 4
THE BUS IS LEAVING!

"Oh, no!" Fergus cried. "The bus is here, and I am not in Emma's backpack. How will I ever get home?"

"Follow me," Zeke said. "Maybe we can make it back before the bus leaves."

So they ran through the old-smelling dinosaur bones. "Good-bye, dinosaurs!" Fergus called. "I have to go home!"

They ran through the butterfly garden.

"Good-bye, butterflies!" Fergus called.

"I have to go home!"

They raced past the lions and gorillas.

Where were Emma and Lucy and Miss
Maxwell?

GORILLA

"This way!" cried Zeke. "It's a shortcut!"
They rushed through a room full of
insects and spiders and ran down a hallway
with a big door at the end. Could it lead
back to the coatroom?

Beyond the door, it was dark. Black as night. There were stars on the ceiling. The planetarium!

Fergus looked up at the imaginary sky just as a shooting star streaked past. He wished as hard as he could. *Let me find Emma and Lucy and Miss Maxwell. I want to go home!*

Just then, another door cracked open,
and light spilled into the dark. "Over there!"
Zeke cried.

They zipped out the door, down a
hallway, and into a crowded room. People
were standing in line and sitting on benches.

And there was Emma's backpack!
Fergus was so excited he did his jazzy dance,
right there in the lobby. "I'm going home!"
he cried. "Back to the classroom and stories
and music and art!"

"Won't you miss dinosaurs and butterflies and stars? What about lion taming and high-climbing adventures?" said Zeke.

"We have adventures in the classroom, too," Fergus said. "Especially at storytime."

"What about friends?" Zeke said. "I can't be king of the beasts all by myself."

"I have an idea," Fergus said. "Come with me!" They climbed into Emma's backpack just as the children lined up for the bus.

"Everyone be sure to sit with your buddy!" said Miss Maxwell. And Fergus did.

"We should get out of this backpack and jump on the seats!" Zeke said.

Fergus shook his head. He'd had enough trouble for one day.

"You have to stay in your seat on the bus," he told Zeke. "That's a rule for people and mice. Miss Maxwell has rules in her classroom, too. You will need to follow them."

Zeke made a face. "I don't like following rules. But I do like having a friend."
He smiled at Fergus. "So I promise I'll do my best." And that was good enough for Fergus.

When they got back to school, Emma put her backpack on her desk.

"It's time to go home now," Miss Maxwell told the class. Fergus and Zeke didn't have far to go.

As the students were getting ready to leave, Jake looked into the mouse cage. "Miss Maxwell, Fergus has a friend!"

All the children gathered around.

"He's cute," said Emma.

"And friendly," said Jake.

"Where'd he come from?" asked Lucy.

"I'd say we have a bit of a mystery," said Miss Maxwell.

"I'd say we have a new class pet," said Emma.